BURIED
TREASURE

By Marcia Thornton Jones and Debbie Dadey

Illustrated by Amy Wummer

Hyperion Books for Children
New York

To four special dog lovers: Becky Dadey, Lindsay Stoltz, Halley Baker, and Kelsey Hinton

—DD

To the members of my writing group; every one a true treasure: Lynne Brandon, Marnie Brooks, Laurie Calkhoven, Candy Dahl, Cathy Dubowski, Martha Levine, Joanne Nicoll, Becky Rector, Mara Rockliff, Katrina Schmitz, Susan Spain, Barbara Underhill. RAH!

—MTJ

Printed in the United States of America
First Edition
1 3 5 7 9 10 8 6 4 2
Book design by Dawn Adelman
This book is set in 14-pt. Cheltenham.
ISBN 0-7868-1675-9
Visit www.barkleyschool.com

Contents

BAD NEWS

My human Maggie dropped me off at Barkley's School for Dogs just as Blondie and her human walked in the door.

With her curly white hair and big brown eyes, Blondie was the best-looking pooch at Barkley's. She was also one of my best friends. "Good to see you, Jack," Blondie said to me in dog talk.

It's a Fido Fact that all dogs understand people, but people can't understand dog talk.

"Hi, Blondie," I said with a grin on my

face. But Woodrow and Bubba got rid of my smile quicker than a dog can eat a treat.

"*Shh,*" said my little pup friend, Bubba.

"Listen," Woodrow, the smartest old basset hound around, said. "Something is wrong."

I perked up my ears. I don't like to brag, but I consider myself a Wonder Dog, and my hearing is better than the average dog's. On the other side of the front room I saw my beagle buddy, Floyd.

Floyd dangled a red rubber bone from his mouth as he stared at his human, a burly man with big ears. "Yep," Floyd's human told Fred Barkley. "It looks like I'll be getting that new job. I'm making my decision today."

My tail stopped wagging and drooped all the way to the floor. Blondie gasped, and Floyd dropped his chew toy. The humans didn't notice.

3

"Congratulations, you're moving up in the world," Fred told Floyd's human.

"I'm keeping my fingers crossed," the man said and patted Floyd on the head. "And wherever I go, Floyd is going with me."

Woodrow barked. "Move? Did he say *move*?"

"Oh, no," Blondie said with a whine. "Floyd is moving?"

Sweetcakes, the meanest and biggest Doberman pinscher I had ever met,

chuckled from behind Fred Barkley. "I'm glad Floyd's moving," Sweetcakes said. "That's one less dog around here. In fact, I hope all you dogs move so I can have this place to myself." Sweetcakes belonged to Fred Barkley, the owner of our school. Sweetcakes wasn't crazy about sharing her human and her home with the rest of us.

"Yeah, yeah," Clyde panted from beside Sweetcakes. "Move, move." Sometimes I wondered if Clyde was glued to

Sweetcakes's side. Wherever Sweetcakes went, Clyde tagged along. They were like Batman and Robin, except that Sweetcakes and Clyde weren't the good guys.

The thought of Floyd moving left me speechless, which is pretty unusual for a Wonder Dog like me. I am well known for quality barking, if I do say so myself.

Floyd was one of the first friends I had made when I first started at Barkley's. He couldn't really be moving. Could he?

BANDIT

"Wait just a doggone minute," I said when we were out in the play yard. "Floyd can't be moving."

The yard at Barkley's was filled with toys made just for dogs. There were tunnels and balance beams and bars to jump over. There was even a seesaw. But those things didn't interest us one bit. We were too worried about what we had over-heard.

"It sounds like my human really wants to move," Floyd said. His tail drooped to

7

the ground, and his forehead wrinkled in a frown.

Woodrow opened his mouth to say something, but he didn't get a chance because the back door swung open wide. A new dog pranced into the Barkley's School play yard.

"Hi!" the new dog yipped. "I'm Petey." Petey was a wiggly little white Jack Russell terrier. He didn't stand still for more than two wags of a dog's tail.

Floyd lowered his head even more. "I guess Petey will be my replacement, now that I'm leaving."

"You can't move," I told Floyd firmly. "We'll think of some way for you to stay."

"I have to go where my human goes," Floyd said sadly. "It looks like this is my last day at Barkley's." He wandered over to Woodrow's pile of rags and curled up for a nap.

"Poor Floyd," Woodrow said. "I don't want to see him go."

"I don't want to see the mess that new pup is making," Blondie said as she watched Petey start digging holes in the ground. "Fred is going to blame us."

Blondie was right. Petey was wild. He ran around the play yard, sniffing as if treats were hidden in the grass. When he wasn't sniffing, he was digging. In less than five minutes, Petey had made four holes the size of a dog's rump.

"What's with that dog?" I asked. "Doesn't he know we have a big problem here? We have to figure out how to help Floyd."

Woodrow nodded, his long brown ears swaying alongside him. "Petey reminds me of a dog who went to Barkley's last year. That dog liked to dig, too. He was called Bandit because he stole things and buried them. He even looked like a bandit. He was brown except for black markings on his face like a mask. There was a rumor that some of Bandit's treasure might still be around."

"Treasure?" the little pup, Bubba, asked. He bounded up beside me and wagged his little stub of a tail. "Maybe he buried his treats! Let's find them!"

I shook my head. "I doubt that Bandit buried his treats. Any dog in their right mind would eat his yum-yums right away."

"Maybe Bandit buried chew toys," Blondie suggested. "Most dogs like chew toys."

We all turned to look at Floyd. If there was one thing Floyd loved, it was chew toys, but he wasn't chewing anything now.

Floyd barely lifted his head. I'd never seen him look so sad. "I wish I had a treasure," he whimpered. Then Floyd sighed and dropped his chin to his paws again.

Finding that treasure was one thing that was bound to cheer up the sad hound.

Sweetcakes moved in closer to Floyd. "If there is treasure in this yard," Sweetcakes growled, "it belongs to me."

TREASURE

I shook my head. "Sweetcakes is not going to find that treasure," I said.

"How can you be so sure?" Floyd asked.

I couldn't help but stand a little taller. "Because," I said, "I am going to find it first!"

"How are you going to find buried treasure?" Blondie asked.

"Not to worry," I told her. "I, Jack, the Wonder Dog, will find it."

Blondie looked at me and batted her long eyelashes. "But *how* are you going to find the treasure?" she asked again.

I slumped just a little. I didn't have the slightest idea how to find buried treasure. What could I say? Luckily, Woodrow came to my rescue.

"We have to think of a plan," Woodrow announced.

"Right," Bubba said.

Blondie, Woodrow, Bubba, and I sat for fifteen seconds before Floyd blurted out an idea from his napping spot.

15

"You could look for soft spots in the ground. Whenever I bury something, first I look for soft ground."

"Great idea!" Blondie shouted.

I had to admit that was better than any idea I'd had.

"Let's do it," Bubba shouted. He dashed around the play yard. He tried the dirt under the seesaw, but the dirt was packed hard. He poked his nose under a tunnel, but the tunnel wouldn't budge. Then he found something he could move all by himself.

On the side of the yard, next to the tall brick wall, there were four metal trash cans. Before I could stop him, Bubba dashed across the yard and jumped up, his two puppy paws against one of the trash cans. It tipped into the trash can next to it. Then both of the cans tilted into the third. *CRASH!* They all toppled and tumbled to the ground.

"I found a perfect spot!" Bubba yipped. Dirt flew everywhere as Bubba dug like an octopus with eight shovels. Bubba hadn't just found a soft spot. He had found mud—gooey mud that a pup could really sink his paws into.

Soon, Bubba's paws were caked with mud, and he had a hole big enough to stick his head into, all the way up to his ears. When he pulled out his head, there was a round blob of mud perched on his nose.

"I found something!" Bubba barked.

JACK THE PIRATE

"Is it the treasure?" Floyd asked. The idea of finding treasure made Floyd look a little happier. "Did Bubba find the treasure?"

"There's only one way to find out," I said. I leaped across the yard. Blondie and Woodrow were hot on my tail. Even Floyd perked up. He stood up, shook himself all the way down to his tail, and hurried over to see what Bubba had found.

"Did you find something good?" Blondie asked.

Bubba nodded. His tongue hung out the side of his mouth and the sound of his tail hitting the fallen trash cans sounded like a racing heartbeat. "This is great. It's wonderful!" Bubba panted.

"What is it?" Woodrow asked.

Bubba stepped aside and we crowded around the hole to peer inside. "I see three worms, a snail, and a bug with six legs," Woodrow finally announced.

Bubba hopped up and down. "I know,"

he said. "Aren't they great?"

I had to smile. Being a pup, Bubba sometimes got a little too excited.

Blondie patted Bubba on the back. "Bugs are a nice find, but I don't think it's Bandit's treasure."

"No," Floyd said. His tail stopped wagging and it dropped to the ground. "That's not the treasure." Then he headed back to the pile of rags. He turned around three times and settled in as if he never planned to get up.

Bubba was too excited to notice Floyd was feeling as if he'd just lost his favorite chew toy. "If Bandit's treasure is better than this, then I have to keep digging," Bubba said, and he was off at a full gallop across the yard. Bubba already had dirt all over his legs and nose. His color changed from black to dirt brown.

Bubba wasn't the only one with dirty paws. Petey was still digging holes everywhere. He'd dig for a few minutes with his white tail wagging. Then he'd sniff and try another spot. Petey didn't seem to care that he didn't find anything, he just liked digging. He dug beside tunnels and under the teeter-totter. The play yard was definitely getting messy, and Petey's piles of dirt were everywhere.

Sweetcakes didn't like getting her toenails dirty. She just followed Petey around. Whenever Petey left a hole, Sweetcakes made Clyde dig the hole deeper, just to make sure there wasn't any treasure inside. "Dig, dig," Clyde panted.

I had to admit, something deep down inside me wanted to dig, too. But I knew Fred Barkley would not like the idea of a million holes appearing in the yard. There had to be a better way to discover Bandit's hiding place.

So, I used my brain instead of my paws.

I went to Woodrow. He had settled in next to Floyd for a nap. If any dog knew what to do, it would be Woodrow. After all, he was the oldest dog at Barkley's. He was also a basset hound, and bassets are known to be serious trail dogs.

"Hey, Woodrow," I whispered. "Can you remember where Bandit liked to dig?"

Woodrow's forehead was always a little wrinkled, but it wrinkled even more when he thought about something. Finally, he shook his head. "Maybe thinking like a pirate would help," Woodrow suggested. "It might give us ideas."

Bubba bounded past just as Woodrow spoke. "Pirate? What's a pirate?"

I knew about pirates from watching movies with my human. I stepped up to explain. "A pirate is a thief on water," I told the pup.

"A bathtub thief? Do they steal rubber duckies?" Bubba asked.

24

I understood Bubba's confusion. After all, he was a pup of only a few months, and the most water he had ever seen was at home in the bathtub. I couldn't expect him to know as much as a Wonder Dog like me.

"Pirates wore eye patches and bandannas around their heads," I explained, as I remembered the movies I'd seen. "They traveled in big ships that floated on water as far as a pup's eye could see. They were no-good thieves who would find other boats in the water and jump on board. Then, they would steal anything and everything before sailing off again."

I closed one eye as if it were covered by a patch. "Ahoy, matey. There be treasure ahead!" I growled in my best pirate voice.

Bubba laughed and then darted between my legs. "I want to play pirate," he said as he tried to close one eye, too.

At first, Blondie, Woodrow, and Floyd

looked at us as if we were one pup short of a litter. But soon they were laughing along with us. Even Floyd's tail was wagging over our pirate game. We were so busy having fun, we forgot about digging. We even forgot about Bandit's treasure. And we definitely forgot about one very big and very mean Doberman pinscher.

"I found the treasure!" Sweetcakes suddenly roared, "and it's mine. All mine!"

SWEETCAKES'S TREASURE

"Oh, no," Bubba whined. "We're too late."

Sweetcakes dove straight into one of the holes Petey had started. Her huge rump with its short little tail stuck up high in the air.

"Sweetcakes's treasure," Clyde panted as Sweetcakes rooted in the hole.

"This is terrible," Floyd said with a frown. "Sweetcakes found the treasure."

The news *was* terrible. If Sweetcakes found the treasure before the rest of us,

BANDIT

PETEY

FiDo FACTS

● ● ● ● ● ● ● ● ● ● ● ● ● ●

name: Petey

Breed: Jack Russell terrier

Size: Small

Favorite trick: Digging holes the fastest

Characteristics: Perky, devoted, merry

Art © 2002 by Amy Wummer
From Barkley's School for Dogs #7 **Buried Treasure**
© 2002 VOLO

FiDo FACTS

● ● ● ● ● ● ● ● ● ● ● ● ● ●

name: Bandit

Breed: Mixed breed

Size: Medium

Favorite trick: Hiding his treats

Characteristics: Mysterious, sly, lively

Art © 2002 by Amy Wummer
From Barkley's School for Dogs #7 **Buried Treasure**
© 2002 VOLO

DOG-GONE FUN

● ● ● ● ● ● ● ● ● ● ● ● ● ●

Dog-eared Delight

Give yourself a pair of dog ears! Measure and cut out a long strip of paper that will fit around your head. Staple or tape the ends together. now cut out a pair of dog ears and paste them on the sides. The ears can be long and floppy like Woodrow's or pointy like Jack's. Decorate and color, and soon you'll have a canine crown!

Art © 2002 by Amy Wummer
From Barkley's School for Dogs #7 **Buried Treasure**
© 2002 VOLO

BE A TOP DOG

● ● ● ● ● ● ● ● ● ● ● ● ● ●

After reading the book, try answering these questions:

1. Where is the treasure buried?

2. Who is the newest dog at Barkley's?

3. Which dog might move away?

4. What is in the treasure box?

1. Behind the shed 2. Petey 3. Floyd 4. Steak bones

Art © 2002 by Amy Wummer
From Barkley's School for Dogs #7 **Buried Treasure**
© 2002 VOLO

she would brag about it until every ear at Barkley's was sore just from listening.

Woodrow shook his head, letting his long ears drag across the ground. "Maybe she found that treasure, and maybe she didn't. Let's find out for sure."

We reached Sweetcakes just as she tugged what she had found out of the hole. Sweetcakes dropped it to the ground for us all to see.

"A rock?" Floyd said with a little laugh. "Sweetcakes found a rock!"

The smile disappeared from Floyd's face when Sweetcakes towered over him and snarled. "Too bad it's your last day here," she growled. Then she marched away from us all.

We stared at the rock, but we thought about what Sweetcakes had said. Floyd's time at Barkley's was short. The idea of Floyd leaving was far worse than not finding Bandit's treasure.

Bubba tried to wipe some of the dirt off his nose. "A rock is better than nothing," he said with his little puppy voice.

"But a treasure would be better," Floyd told my friends.

I nudged Floyd's back. "Having you stay would be the best thing of all," I said quietly so no one but Floyd could hear.

Floyd smiled just a bit. "Thanks, Jack."

Meanwhile, Bubba sniffed the air.

31

"Maybe we haven't found the treasure because it's covered," he suggested.

"Of course it's covered," I said with a patient smile. "It's under the ground."

"Wait," Woodrow said. "Bubba has an idea. The treasure must be someplace hard to get to. Someplace a dog wouldn't think to look. Someplace that isn't very obvious."

"Exactly," Bubba said, his tail already going so fast it became a blur. "Someplace like under the tunnel!"

We all looked at the long red tube in the center of the yard. I had spent plenty of times zipping through it, but I had never once given a thought to what might lie beneath it. Bubba's idea suddenly made sense. It would be the perfect hiding place.

"Come on, Jack," Bubba yelped as he hopped over spilled garbage to the tunnel. Help me push this over."

I leaped across the yard, not worrying about the spilled trash that I scattered. We used our shoulders and shoved at the plastic. The tunnel started to roll. "Harder," Bubba said as Floyd and Blondie came to help. I hopped up, put two muddy paws on the side of the tunnel, and gave a Wonder Dog shove. The tunnel rolled out of the way. I stomped on the spot where the tunnel used to be. It was as hard as a three-year-old dog biscuit.

Bubba shrugged. "I guess that wasn't such a good idea after all."

Fred Barkley walked out the back door, took one look at the yard, and stopped dead in his tracks. "Who made this mess?" Fred shouted.

There I stood next to the muddy tunnel, my paws full of mud, and trash scattered around me. I knew it didn't look good. I tilted my head and gave Fred my most innocent look. It didn't work.

"It's time out for you," Fred said, pulling me behind the shed.

Sweetcakes snickered as Fred pulled me past her. "I'll find that treasure right after I get my treats," she barked to me.

"Whatever you do," I yelped to my friends, "don't let Sweetcakes dig for the treasure."

Things were looking pretty bleak, but then something happened to make things worse.

SOUR PUSS

Time-out is in the back of the yard, behind the shed, in a quiet corner. Fred makes us stay there, all alone, when he thinks we need to settle down. Every dog dreads it, none more than me. I know. I've been in time-out before.

I watched Fred disappear around the corner of the shed. I could hear him start lessons with the other dogs. I sighed and lay down, ready for a long, lonely wait.

"So, what did you do this time?" a sassy voice asked.

I knew that voice and it meant my day had just gone from bad to doggone-awful. I closed my eyes. Tight. Maybe if I ignored her she would just go away.

"I said, what did you do this time?"

I flopped over on my side and opened one eye. There, sprawled on top of the brick wall surrounding our yard, was a fat black-and-gold cat. This was not just any cat. This was Tazz. Tazz lived in my

apartment building, and she had a bad habit of showing up at the very worst times. Like now. She stared at me with her yellow eyes, swishing her bushy tail lazily back and forth.

"Go away," I snapped. It's not exactly true that all dogs hate cats. In fact, I think cats are just fine—as long as they're far away from me. But something about seeing that bushy tail hanging just out of my reach was making my nose itch and my paws quiver.

"Cheer up," Tazz nearly purred. "Nobody likes a sourpuss."

"You should know." I must admit I growled. After all, being a cat, she was the sourest puss of all.

Tazz stood up, her tail making a lazy swirl high in the air. She walked along the top of the wall until she cast a shadow over me.

"Now, listen here," she told me. "Just

because you are having a bad day, it doesn't mean you can be snappy."

I sighed. I hated to admit to a cat that she was right, but it was the truth. "Sorry," I mumbled. "It's been a dog-awful day."

Tazz wiped her long whiskers with a paw before saying anything else. Finally she stopped, paw in midair, and winked one yellow eye.

"You're having a hard time finding that

treasure, aren't you?" she purred.

"How would you know?" I asked. Tazz had a habit of sticking her nose where it didn't belong.

"I've been watching. In fact, I know a thing or two about the dogs at Barkley's."

I hopped up and growled. It wasn't a little growl, either. It's a Fido Fact that dogs don't like sassy cats spying on them. I intended to tell Tazz right then and there, but she didn't give me a chance.

"Listen to what I have to say," Tazz hissed. "The dogs at Barkley's will never find that treasure unless they work together."

"Listen to a cat?" I howled. "A Wonder Dog would never listen to a cat! Never!"

TiRED

I was ready to show Tazz just how serious a Wonder Dog could be. Lucky for her, Fred interrupted our little conversation. Just as Fred strode around the shed, Tazz slipped to the other side of the wall.

I barked to get her attention.

"Shh," Fred said. He said that to me all the time, so I didn't listen to him. Instead, I barked again.

I don't think Tazz heard me, but Fred sure did. He knelt down on the ground, held my mouth closed, and looked me straight in the eyes. Fred is a good person. After all, he likes dogs. But there's something about people's big, furless noses that make me want to look the other way. So I did. That didn't stop Fred.

"Jack," he said, "you must learn to be a good dog."

Fred's words hurt me down to the tip of my tail. After all, I was better than good. I was a Wonder Dog.

Fred scratched my left ear, exactly where I like to be scratched. "I know you don't mean any harm," he said. "You're just full of energy. What you need is to join everyone else in lessons."

I was glad Fred wasn't too mad at me, so I wagged my tail.

"See," Fred said, "you like the idea of a good workout."

"What? Workout?" I asked, only I said it in dog talk, so Fred didn't understand. It was too late, anyway. Fred slapped his thigh and told me to heel. He's always talking about his feet, so I did what any Wonder Dog would do. I sniffed his toes.

"That's a good dog," Fred said as he led me around the edge of the shed. Then he whistled for the rest of the dogs to line up.

All the dogs trotted over to Fred. Petey was so excited he ran across the yard and hopped right into Fred's arms.

"That's the spirit, Petey," Fred said. "Let's all get ready for a little fun."

I scanned the yard for Sweetcakes. She crouched beneath the teeter-totter. Since Fred was her human, she didn't like any other dog to get too close to him. I wondered how she liked the idea of the new pup being snuggled in Fred's arms. By the look on her face, she didn't like it one bit.

Sweetcakes came over to Fred and let him rub her tattered ear. Fred didn't even notice when Sweetcakes snapped at

Petey's hind foot. Petey just smiled.

Fred put his whistle to his mouth and blew. Every dog lined up beside a row of striped tires hung from stands. "This is a new lesson," he told us. "You're going to love it."

Sweetcakes demonstrated first, of course. Sweetcakes had seen the tires before, no doubt about it. She hopped through the tires without snagging a single toenail.

Bubba went next. He had great fun hopping around—but he kept missing the middle of the tires and ended up rolling on the ground.

Woodrow stepped up to the tires, took one sniff, and then headed back. Woodrow had been at Barkley's so long, Fred didn't mind. Floyd went next, but I could see that his heart wasn't really in it.

Blondie, being the perfect dog that she

was, daintily hopped through each and every hole.

I tried to follow her, but it was taking too long. I missed the last tire and landed right in front of Fred. If you ask me, it doesn't make much sense to hop through the middle of them, anyway.

Petey took one look at the row of tires and decided burrowing under them was much more fun than hopping over them. He dove under a tire and started wiggling and squirming until he found the perfect digging spot. Rhett and Scarlett, the two Irish setters, stepped out of line to watch before Fred could stop them. Harry the Westie darted between Rhett and Scarlett and dove under one of the tires, too.

In no time flat, the tires were a mess, and Fred was—well, he was tired.

Fred blew his whistle and every dog stopped midstep. "Enough!" Fred yelled. He dug in his pocket and pulled out a bag

of treats. "You all worked hard, so you each deserve a yum-yum," he said. As I said, Fred is a pretty decent human. He knows what dogs like. We crowded around Fred.

I was so busy savoring the last bite of my treat that I didn't notice what was happening just three tail-lengths away until it was almost too late.

THE ONE AND
ONLY REASON

For the first time that day, Petey didn't look so peppy. That's because Sweetcakes and Clyde had Petey backed into a corner. Petey's treat sat between Sweetcakes's dirty paws.

"Keep digging holes," Sweetcakes snarled at Petey.

"Yeah," Clyde said. "Dig, dig."

"And don't stop until I find that treasure," Sweetcakes added.

I felt sorry for the new pup. After all, Petey hadn't hurt a flea. He had been so busy digging his holes, he didn't even know that the rest of us were caught in a treasure-hunt struggle. But now Petey was finding out the score, and by the looks of his shaking legs, I could tell he didn't like it one bit.

He looked up into Sweetcakes's face and nodded. "I . . . I like to d-dig holes," Petey stammered.

"Good," Sweetcakes said. "Because you

won't get another treat until I find that treasure." Sweetcakes swallowed up Petey's treat in one big bite. "Now, dig!"

Petey yelped and darted under Sweetcakes's belly. His little legs attacked the dirt as he started to dig. Sweetcakes towered over him, waiting until the hole was deep. Then she shoved him aside with her nose. "Empty," she told Petey. "You will have to do better than this!"

"Better," Clyde repeated. "Much better."

"We should do something," Blondie said. "It's not fair to poor Petey."

The rest of my friends must have felt the same because they all took one step closer to Sweetcakes. Even Floyd.

"Leave him alone," Floyd said. I must admit, I was amazed. Floyd is not the bravest pup at Barkley's. But today, he wasn't acting like himself. I guess his being sad made him a little braver, too. Unfortunately, it didn't last long.

Sweetcakes glared at Floyd and the rest of us. Then she curled her lip over one of her eyeteeth. "Stay out of this," she growled.

Floyd stepped back. So did Bubba and Blondie. Okay, I admit it, I jumped back a little, too.

We watched Sweetcakes chase Petey from another hole. "Petey is doing what he likes to do," Bubba said with a little whine. "Maybe it's not so bad working with Sweetcakes."

"And Sweetcakes is getting what she wants, too," Woodrow pointed out. "Whether they like it or not, they've just formed a team."

His words made me remember what Tazz had said while I was in time-out. Maybe that cat was right. With Petey's help, Sweetcakes could find the treasure. "We can't let Sweetcakes find that trea-sure!" I barked.

"Too late. Sweetcakes is determined to find it," Blondie said. "Look!"

Sweetcakes chased Petey away before he finished digging one of his holes. Then she reached in with her own paws and started to dig. She was so anxious to find the treasure, she didn't even worry about getting mud between her toenails. Sweetcakes dug, and dug, and dug some more.

Floyd sighed. "I'm sorry we didn't keep

Sweetcakes from digging, but there's nothing we could do."

I looked at Floyd. Usually, my buddy was full of energy, ready to chew on any toy within reach. Not today. He was too sad. "Don't worry, Floyd," I told him. "We'll think of something."

For a brief moment, Floyd smiled. "No matter where I go, I'll never forget you," he said. "After all, who could forget a Wonder Dog!"

I smiled. "You're one of the best friends a dog could ever want. I'll never forget you, either. After all, no dog is better at fetching than you."

"Thanks, Jack," Floyd said. "It helps just knowing you're my friend. But it would be nice to be remembered for more than fetching—something like finding Bandit's treasure."

At first, Floyd's words made my heart swell. He really believed I was a Wonder

Dog. That good feeling didn't last long. If I really was the Wonder Dog at Barkley's, how could I let my friend down? I knew what I had to do. And I couldn't do it alone.

My friends and I had to find that treasure before Sweetcakes did. Not because we wanted it. Not because we wanted to beat Sweetcakes. The one and only reason we had to find the treasure was for Floyd. We had to do it for our friend!

THE REAL
WONDER DOG

"We're going make your last day at Barkley's the best day you ever had," I told Floyd and the rest of my friends.

"Impossible," Floyd said. "This is the saddest day I'll ever know."

"Until now, it has been," I said with a nod. "But it's about to get better, because we're going to find that treasure."

"How do you plan to do that?" Woodrow asked.

I smiled. Usually Woodrow had all the answers, but today I was the one who knew what to do. Remembering what Tazz the cat had said, I told my friends, "I am not going to find it. We are. Together!"

"I want to help, I want to help!" Bubba begged.

"Everyone is going to help," I said. "We are going to work as a team!"

For the first time ever, Woodrow actually looked excited. He hopped up and turned in a complete circle. "Fabulous idea!" he said.

Blondie batted her eyelashes and

nodded. "It's fang-tastic!" she said with a smile.

Floyd grinned. "I'd say it's dog-awesome!"

"Then let's get to work," I told them.

We surveyed the yard. We had to find Bandit's hiding place.

Petey and Sweetcakes were busy digging holes in the middle of the play yard. Bubba had already explored under the trash cans. "Think," I said.

Dogs do many things well. We dig. We bark. We chase sticks. But thinking is not always so easy. That didn't stop us. We put our heads together. "What do we know about Bandit?" I asked.

"He lived here a long time ago," Bubba said.

"He was brown with black markings on his face," Blondie remembered.

"He stole things and dug lots of holes," Floyd added.

I nodded, trying to imagine Bandit racing around the yard at Barkley's, digging his many holes. I couldn't help but think Bandit must have been a little silly. After all, I knew how Fred had acted when he thought I had dug the holes and knocked over the trash cans. Bubba must have been thinking the very same thing.

"You know," the little pup said, "I bet Bandit was always in trouble."

"That's it!" I barked. "That's it! That's it! Bandit was always in trouble! That can mean only one thing!"

"What?" Floyd asked.

"Follow me, and I'll show you where Bandit hid his treasure!" I told them.

I made sure Sweetcakes wasn't watching, then I led my friends along the brick wall and around the shed.

"I don't like it back here," Bubba said. "This is the time-out place."

I grinned. "Exactly," I said. "Few dogs

come back here unless they have to. If Bandit was always in trouble, he spent a lot of time back here. Time enough to find the perfect spot to bury his loot!"

Woodrow nodded. "I think you may have something," he said. "In fact, I think you are right on target. And I bet the perfect spot is that corner right behind the shed."

We all looked. Sure enough, there was a mound of dirt. "Let's go," I barked.

I started to dig. But soon Floyd, Woodrow, and Bubba pitched in to help. Even Blondie got her pretty white paws dirty. We took turns digging. Whenever one dog got tired, another took over. I had my head deep in a hole when I finally scratched something. Something hard! It had to be Bandit's treasure. My paws were itching to dig some more. I could just imagine clamping my Wonder Dog jaws around whatever was buried in that hole.

But I didn't do it. Instead, I jumped out of the hole and told Floyd it was his turn to dig.

"I'll dig," Bubba offered. "I'm not too tired."

I shook my head and gently nudged Bubba away from the hole. "This hole is a little too deep for a pup like you. I think Floyd's the hound for the job."

Floyd stepped up to the hole. He had

only dug for a second when he shouted, "I found it!"

Bubba yipped. Woodrow peered into the hole. Not Blondie. She took a step closer to me and whispered in my ear. "You let him find it, didn't you?"

I slowly shook my head. "Floyd found that treasure," was all I said.

Blondie said, "You truly are a Wonder Dog."

I started to point out that Floyd was the real Wonder Dog, but I was rudely interrupted by a big growl. That growl could only belong to one dog at Barkley's.

Sweetcakes.

FAIR AND SQUARE

"Give me my treasure," Sweetcakes growled.

"Yeah, yeah," Clyde panted. "Treasure, treasure."

The hair on my back stood up. I wasn't about to let Sweetcakes get Floyd's treasure. "That's not yours," I snarled. "Floyd found it fair and square."

"It's mine now," Sweetcakes said, moving so close I could feel her hot breath.

I wanted to back away, but I didn't. "You can't have it," I said.

"Who is going to stop me?" Sweetcakes snapped.

"I will," I said. I knew that Sweetcakes would probably tear off my ears, but how could I let Sweetcakes take Floyd's treasure?

For the second time that day, Floyd did something very brave. He stepped between Sweetcakes and me. He held his black nose high and said, "Let

Sweetcakes have the treasure. No treasure is worth my friend getting hurt over."

Sweetcakes grinned so that her yellow teeth showed. Then Sweetcakes jumped in the hole after the treasure. I wanted to jump in after her, but Floyd held me back. "It's okay," Floyd said.

Sweetcakes pulled. She tugged. She growled. She even whined. But no matter what she did, Sweetcakes could not budge the treasure box in the hole.

The rest of the dogs peered over the edge of the hole. Finally, Floyd cleared his throat, and for the third time in one day, he shocked us all.

"You know," Floyd said, "if we all worked together we could share whatever is in that box."

Sweetcakes glared up at Floyd. Mud covered her nose and she was panting from working so hard.

All the other dogs backed away from Sweetcakes and Clyde. All of them except Floyd, Woodrow, and me.

Sweetcakes growled again. "Share?" Sweetcakes said with a snarl. "Me share with *you*?"

"Share? Share?" Clyde repeated.

Floyd nodded. "You do know what that means, don't you? We help you get that box out of the ground, and we all share what's inside. It's either that or we can all turn around and leave you sitting in that hole for Fred Barkley to find you. Then *you'll* end up in time-out for digging a hole the size of a cow."

"Time-out, time-out," Clyde panted. He hopped from one foot to another he was so nervous.

Sweetcakes was not known for sharing, but she had never been in time-out. Well, almost never. "The treasure is no good to any of us if it stays in this hole," Sweetcakes finally said. "I suppose we could give Floyd's idea a try."

I couldn't believe we were actually teaming up with Sweetcakes, but that's exactly what we did. Floyd and I, with the help of Sweetcakes, broke the box free from the mud and dragged it out of the hole.

We stood there, panting, the box in front of us. Floyd was the first to catch his breath. He lifted his nose, and with his beautiful beagle howl, he announced that

whatever was in the chest was for all the dogs of Barkley's to share. "We all worked for what's in this box," he said. "Fair and square!"

Then Floyd lifted the lid. It truly was a dog's treasure chest—full of bones!

"Old steak bones! My favorite!" yipped Bubba.

Floyd made sure every pup in the yard had a bone to gnaw for our own little bone party.

The end of the school day came soon after that. Too soon. Floyd's human was the first to arrive. He came outside to talk to Fred, who was working extra hard trying to fill in all the holes in the yard.

We gathered around Floyd, saying good-bye. "Finding the treasure today was great," Floyd said. "You are all the best friends that I've ever had."

"Wait," Woodrow said. "Listen."

Floyd's human was talking to Fred. "That job didn't turn out, after all," Fred's human said. "I just couldn't stand the idea of leaving everything behind. And I know Floyd would hate to leave Barkley's."

They said some more things, but we couldn't hear them because Bubba was running in circles and yipping. Well, I might as well tell you the whole truth. I let out a few glorious barks, too.

ABOUT THE AUTHORS

Marcia Thornton Jones and Debbie Dadey used to work together at the same elementary school—Marcia taught in the classroom and Debbie was a librarian. But now they love writing about a totally different kind of school . . . where the students have four legs and a tail!

Marcia lives in Lexington, Kentucky, and Debbie lives in Fort Collins, Colorado. Their own pets have inspired them to write about Jack and his friends at Barkley's School. These authors have also written The Adventures of the Bailey School Kids, The Bailey City Monsters, and the Triplet Trouble series together.